LOCAL
LEGENDS
OF
COSTA RICA

EXPLORING COSTA RICA THROUGH FOLKLORE

PRATEEK AGRAWAL

ISBN: 979-8-389190-71-9

Disclaimer

The author writes from his own personal experience
travelling various places in Costa Rica and meeting locals.
Not all beliefs, stories or scientific explanations may be
agreed upon by everybody. It is not the intent of the
author to hurt anyone's sentiments or discredit anyone's
research.

Sometimes I wish I could be,

A wave that flows upon the sea.

No barriers to keep me at bay,

I'll swim away! I'll swim away!

Going wherever I please,

A life of ease! A life of ease!

CONTENTS

PREFACE

The makings of this book originated in a quiet, cozy coffee shop in the foothills of Tenorio Volcano when I was on my way to see, for the first time, the fabled crystal blue waters of Rio Celeste. I was full of anticipation for the day ahead. I had seen the pictures online, read articles, and I was eager to see the river for myself.

As I drank my coffee, I had a lovely conversation with the owners of the cafe – a sweet elderly lady and her son – about my plans for the day. They were all too happy to tell me about the significance of the area that surrounded us, and in particular, the mythical beauty of Rio Celeste. While I talked to them, I realized that Rio Celeste holds much more significance in their eyes than just its famously electric-blue coloring.

To them, this place is not about tourism surrounding the

stunning scenery. Instead, it is about the place's origin story – not just history in the textbook sense. Costa Rica is full of folklore passed down through storytelling, songs, and legends, all interconnected with the beliefs of the indigenous people who still live there today. That lore flows through the waters of Rio Celeste, glows at the belly of the Arenal volcano, and flies through the trees of the country's lush cloud forests.

Preserving this vibrant history is a complex task, the cafe owners told me, which is focused not just on saving the rich biodiversity supported by the wild landscapes of Costa Rica, but also on sharing the elaborate folklore and storytelling that wraps around so many of Costa Rica's landmarks and locations. Passing through generations, Costa Rica's folklore could be traced back to the ancient beliefs of the very people who first called this place their home. Without preserving the underlying history of these locations, visitors and locals alike would miss out on a huge part of what makes Costa Rica unique.

I came away from that conversation with a thorough appreciation of how much folklore and mythology can add to the experience of a place. Learning about it can help answer many questions that may run through our heads, including the main question I asked on that day:

Why is the water in Rio Celeste this kind of crystal blue?

It might sound simple, but in reality, thousands of people have asked this question over time. It's a childlike curiosity that lingers in all of us, as we ask questions such as, "How did that volcano form there?" and "Why does that bird's song sound so different?"

So, why is the water in Rio Celeste crystal blue? Like almost every question in this book, there are two answers: one that appeals to the scientific and logical side of our brains, and the other, which appeals to the part of us that still loves the wild imagination and visualization of childhood…the part that still believes in magic. Costa Rica makes me believe in the existence of magic more than any other place in the world, and it's a feeling that I want to share with others through the stories printed in this book.

During my travels, I have realized that after a place triggers an emotional response inside of you, you are left with a lingering, special connection to that place, no matter how far away from it you may go. You remain linked to that location on some deep level, and over time, your memories of it will morph and change within you. The beauty of that place that you experienced at the moment will evolve from just a

photogenic snapshot to an immersive experience that is "felt" instead of being seen. Whether this experience is the sheer jaw-dropping, breathtaking awe of experiencing a marvel of nature in person, or the joyous memories of a carefree road-trip with your closest friends, these triggered emotions are what make visiting a place truly memorable. While your memories of exactly how a mountain or church looked in the moment may fade, the deep-seated memory of feeling and truly experiencing that location for yourself will stay forever.

I have found that one of the best ways to strengthen this emotional connection and potentially make an experience magical, is to find out more about the history of the place, and the stories that come with it. Dig deep, and you might find something that moves you. It doesn't matter where you are - across the world, regardless of their differences, people love to tell stories. Around every natural wonder and historical location, fables and legends are woven like a blanket, wrapping the present-day in the history of the past.

PURA VIDA

More Than Just A Saying

One cannot understand or even enjoy Costa Rica until one understands *Pura Vida*. This phrase is the most heard one in Costa Rica. The literal translation may be 'Pure Life', but for Costa Ricans, it is a way of life.

Pura Vida is used for everything – everything good, that is. Greeting a friend, bidding farewell, asking for forgiveness, thanking someone, humbly acknowledging someone's appreciation. Letting you know things are 'all good'.

There is a deep significance that lingers underneath these two simple words. It is a constant reminder of a philosophy that encourages peace, being relaxed, and being thankful for what you have instead of lamenting negativity. It is a code to

live life by and is the reason the country consistently ranks high in happiness indexes. Costa Rica also ranks high in average life expectancy. A supplement to diet, exercise, and time spent soaking in the beauty of nature, the low-stress nature of a "Pura Vida" lifestyle contributes to Costa Ricans living longer, better, and free. People leave their offices on time to be with their families. Public parks and recreational centers buzz with activity in the evenings, and couples of all age groups are seen enjoying a night out. People are living purely in the moment.

The phrase is one of the things that unite people in Costa Rica, immigrants and citizens, across race, age, and gender. There's nothing like a sprinkle of Pura Vida to bring communities together and create connections. It's no wonder that for many visitors to the country, the best part of their visit isn't the stunning landscapes, tourist destinations, or action-packed activities – it's the people.

So, has the phrase "Pura Vida" always been so deeply ingrained in Costa Rican culture? Despite its popularity today, "Pura Vida" was only adopted by Costa Ricans fairly recently. Although nobody is completely sure how the term came to be so important to Costa Ricans, the best theory is that it originated from a 1956 film which was titled *Pura Vida!* The film's main character is constantly positive and looks on the

bright side of life, no matter what happens, and uses the saying "Pura Vida" to remind himself of this. By the late 1960s and early 1970s, it was a well-known saying across the nation - and it still is today.

How to make sure that you truly experience the spirit of Pura Vida? This concept isn't something that needs to be forced. Consider it as an opportunity to take a step away from the fast pace of living a modern life, live slowly, and be fully present in each minute that passes. Whether you are at the beach or in a pool, just relax – not only physically, but mentally as well. There is no rush to jump to the next thing, or even think about the next thing.

Life's good right now.

RIO CELESTE

God's Influence In Nature

I n Costa Rica's Tenorio Volcano National Park, you can find a river so deeply blue that photographers are often accused of digitally altering the color in their photos. This river, Rio Celeste, is formed from the union of two other rivers – the Rio Buena Vista, and Quebrada Agria.

Both of the Rio Celeste's parent rivers are relatively colorless, with clear water flowing to the point where they converge. This point of convergence, named El Teñidero, is where the magic of the Rio Celeste becomes obvious to any observer, as the color of the flowing water shifts to an intense, almost neon shade of blue. It's no wonder that the Rio Celeste's name literally translates to "Blue River."

The incredible blue coloring of Rio Celeste has been admired for thousands of years, with people struggling to understand how such an intense shade of blue could occur naturally. Indeed, the appearance of the Rio Celeste is almost otherworldly - and Costa Rican mythology suggests that the river may be truly a spiritual creation. The indigenous people of Costa Rica believe that the intensity of the river's color came from the Gods themselves, at the very creation of the world. Different indigenous tribes hold different beliefs about Gods, but one thing is agreed upon: the color of Rio Celeste is awe-inspiring.

The fable of Rio Celeste's coloring begins with the Gods working to paint the entire sky blue, sweeping large paintbrushes tirelessly and giving color to the world. Like any artist, the time came when the Gods needed to wash their paintbrushes - and so they dipped their brushes in the Rio Celeste to clean them. With every dip of the brushes into the river, the leftover blue paint was washed into the water. After that day, the river would forevermore be the color of the sky. Some believe that the color is most intense in the blue pool at the bottom of Rio Celeste's waterfall because this is the place in the river where the brushes touched the water. Other variations of this origin story believe that stray drops of paint fell into the nearby forest, creating the colorful variety of birds, bugs, and mammals that call the forest home.

Those who have seen the Rio Celeste know that the coloration of the river does not need digital altering or photo filters. To the naked eye, it is just as striking as it appears in photos. So, what exactly causes the dramatic change in color at El Teñidero?

A popular theory was that the color of the Rio Celeste was due to a chemical reaction occurring in the river's waters. Minerals such as copper can lend a bright blue to their surroundings, whereas a chemical reaction between sulfur and calcium carbonate could create a product that would give the river a blue appearance. However, researchers from the University of Costa Rica put this theory to rest by analyzing samples of Rio Celeste's water, which showed low levels of copper and no signs of a colorful chemical reaction. The samples themselves appeared to be as transparent as normal river water as soon as they were transferred into test tubes.

The real answer as to how the Rio Celeste became so strikingly colored seems to lie outside of the river's waters. In fact, the Rio Celeste might appear to be blue due to an optical illusion - meaning that the river's color is created in our own eyes. Because the bottom of the Rio Celeste is covered in a thick layer of white aluminosilicate, rays of light are scattered in different directions when they hit the bottom of the river. This process, called refraction, causes the river to appear a bright shade of blue to our eyes.

If it's just an optical illusion, why does it appear just as intense in photos? Well, cameras were invented to take pictures of what we can see, so camera lenses are modeled after human eyes. If an optical illusion is visible to us, it will usually appear in photos as well. No matter how many beautiful pictures you see online, there is only one way to appreciate the river where the paintbrushes of the gods were washed: by traveling to see it with your own eyes.

TURRIALBA VOLCANO

A Love Story

T he volcanoes of Costa Rica are drenched in rich folklore that tells the story of how these fiery mountains came to be. More often than not, the myths behind Costa Rica's volcanoes are as tumultuous and moving as the volcanoes themselves, and the tale of Turrialba is no exception.

Turrialba is one of the country's five active volcanoes, with multiple eruptions in the past ten years. Despite this violent activity, Turrialba's folklore origin story is soft, sweet, and moving. Sometimes, it has been referred to as the story of Costa Rica's Romeo and Juliet.

The story of Turrialba begins with a tribal chief, who was tragically widowed. His late wife gave him only one daughter, who was named Cira. Cira was beautiful both inside and out, with flowing black hair, and a gentle nature that implored her to show kindness to everyone she met. Despite her soft-heartedness, Cira was a wonderful archer, and her skill with a bow and arrow was unmatched.

Because of Cira's beauty, she had many admirers - but her father, the chief, wished her to marry one man in particular. Cira's husband-to-be was a hunter from the same tribe, who had a handsome face, and was besotted with Cira. The man showered her with gifts to win her heart, but his love for Cira was not returned: her heart had been stolen by another.

Unfortunately, Cira had fallen in love with a man from another tribe, which she knew her father would never approve of. So, she kept her love a secret, deep inside, not even telling her closest confidants. When she crept away at night to visit her lover, she knew that she was risking everything for just one more glimpse of him.

One fateful night, Cira snuck away into the woods to meet with the man she loved. This time, she was not alone. Her father had grown suspicious, as he had noticed that she was disappearing at night and returning in the morning. He ordered several of the tribe's strongest warriors to come with him, and together, they followed Cira in silence.

When Cira's father saw his daughter embracing her lover, he was enraged at his daughter's betrayal and ordered his warriors to shoot Cira and her lover where they stood. Just as the warriors readied their bows, there was an almighty rumble from the earth itself. The young couple's display of true love was so moving that the earth rushed to protect them, opening up a cavern in the ground where they would not be harmed by the arrows. As it grew and grew, the cavern sent out plumes of smoke and lava-hot steam to deflect the tribe's arrows. And so, from the earth's protection of two lovers, Turrialba volcano was born.

This origin story has given Turrialba volcano a romantic reputation, making it a popular location for both locals and tourists. Looking at the volcano, it's easy to daydream about Cira and her love, protected inside the cavern for the rest of eternity. Costa Rican locals will sometimes nudge each other and smile when they see young tourists in love coming to visit Turrialba, knowing that young love has a power that can transcend time.

Visitors to Turrialba are able to walk around the foot of the volcano within the National Park, viewing the ancient lava flows and the forest's scorched areas. However, due to Turrialba's frequent volcanic activity, the park is frequently closed due to volcanic ash or a spike in volcanic activity when the sleeping volcano wakes up.

IRAZU VOLCANO

A Daughter's Devotion

I razu volcano is Costa Rica's tallest active volcano, with multiple craters at the summit, including a stunning crater lake named Diego de la Haya. The volcano's name may come from the words "ara" and "tzu", meaning "point" and "thunder". However, many believe that the name comes from "Iztaru", the name of a neighboring village once located next to the magnificent volcano. However, locals often call Irazu by a different name - "El Coloso"- or "The Colossus" - due to the disasters that the volcano has caused during past eruptions.

Irazu's frequent, violent eruptions seem to match its origin story in Costa Rican mythology. Like Turrialba, the myth of Irazu tells the story of a chief's daughter - but instead of the power of true love, Irazu's origin begins with war.

Legend says that Irazu was born as the daughter of a chief named Aquitaba, and she quickly became his favorite. However, all was not well in Aquitaba's tribe. For years, they had been at war with Guarco, a neighboring village, and the fighting had become so vicious that Aquitaba knew his tribe could not survive for much longer. In his desperation, Aquitaba sent a prayer to the Gods. He was willing to make an enormous sacrifice for peace in the valley where they lived, and although it broke his heart, he knew there was no greater sacrifice than the thing he loved most in the world: his daughter, Irazu.

The Gods agreed to the deal and promised that in exchange for Irazu, they would gift Aquitaba the power to defeat Guarco and end the fight for good. Irazu, who loved her father dearly, wanted nothing more than for the war to end. She was willing to pay the price and agreed to be sacrificed to the Gods. During Aquitaba's next battle with the neighboring village, he prayed to Irazu's spirit, giving thanks and asking for the strength he needed to defeat Guarco.

As Aquitaba finished his prayer, a deep rumble began to emanate from the belly of the tallest mountain in the land. A seam ripped down the center of the mountain, and molten rocks and blasts of fire began to fly toward the enemy village.

The volcanic eruption ended the war, bringing peace to the land - and the Irazu volcano was born.

Irazu has had frequent volcanic eruptions, perhaps because of the restless soul of a sacrificed daughter living within the volcano itself. The volcano has had more than 23 recorded eruptions, with the most famous eruption in 1963 continuing to shower Costa Rica with volcanic ash for two years afterward.

Despite its reputation, Irazu is a very popular tourist destination. Easy to visit and boasting an incredible view of both the Pacific and Atlantic Oceans from the top, Irazu is the perfect example of how the brutality of nature can create incredible beauty.

ARENAL AND LA FORTUNA

Legends from Maleku

I f you wish to see a volcano that looks exactly like the majestic, perfectly triangular image of a volcano in a children's storybook, look no further than Arenal. Unshrouded by land or forest, the striking shape of Arenal can be appreciated from ground level, inspiring a sense of wonder in all observers.

At Arenal's base, there is the town of La Fortuna - "The Fortunate" - which truly embodies the meaning behind its name. Vibrant, full of life and culture, and offering a wide variety of tourist attractions, La Fortuna is not to be missed. The lake at Arenal's foot offers boat rides and tours of the volcano and is popular with both tourists and local sightseers.

Some believe that La Fortuna was given its name because the town was lucky enough to escape damage from the eruptions of Arenal. However, there is no truth to these rumors - in fact, La Fortuna was established long before Arenal's devastating eruptions ravaged the surrounding land. It's more likely that La Fortuna was given its name due to the rest of its luck, in having stunning landmarks and fertile land that created an abundance of food and resources.

Indigenous people, the Maleku, still live in the area surrounding La Fortuna. With the influx of tourists and globalization, the Maleku constantly strive to preserve their culture, traditions, and language for the next generation. With Arenal looming over the village and the constant awareness of any activity in the volcano, it's no wonder that the Maleku believe that the volcano is more than just a pile of rock - in fact, the striking volcano is the home of one of their Gods, Tocú.

Legend has it that Tocú's home inside the body of Arenal is the reason why the Maleku came to the area in the first place. By living close to their God, it was possible to escape his rages of fury and appease him by interpreting his messages. Each rumble from the belly of Arenal is Tocú's way of sending a message to the Maleku, and only the tribe's elders are wise and experienced enough to decipher what the message may be. In the same way, the only people who are permitted to reply to Tocú are the elders.

Each flow of lava from Arenal conveyed a message from Tocú, warning the Maleku of a catastrophic event that was about to happen, or making a show of strength to prove Tocú's total dominion over the land. In exchange for these warnings and protection, Tocú demanded that the Maleku provide him with total devotion and respect for the higher, more-sacred parts of the volcano. For a time, the Maleku lived in relative peace.

The peace was shattered with the arrival of invaders, who began to destroy the forest around Arenal and fought with the Maleku. Tocú was enraged to witness these events, which had killed his worshippers and damaged the flourishing nature around Arenal. His anger brought forth plumes of fiery gas, and rocks which he threw into the air with great force. After hearing about the destruction that Tocú was causing, the Maleku were able to convince the invading tribe to leave the area peacefully. After this, the Maleku were able to soothe Tocú into easing his destruction, and the time of peace returned.

Today, the Maleku share their culture and beliefs with tourists, opening their lands to allow a steady flow of visitors, and selling their unique crafts, art, and locally grown produce. Up until 2010, Arenal was considered to be the most active volcano in Costa Rica. However, since then, the flow of volcanic ash and lava from the volcano has ceased, and Arenal is now considered to be "sleeping." Perhaps Tocú is enjoying a sense of peace in the land - but if there's anything that Costa Rica's legends tell us, it is that a sleeping God can always be woken.

BARVA

Greed and Broken Promises

As a contrast to some of the more volatile Costa Rican volcanoes, the sleepy giant of Barva is still worth visiting. With no recorded volcanic activity for over 8000 years, the trails around Barva offer tourists a hike in the lush, green forest, and the quiet observance of the eerily quiet lake at the volcano's base.

Unlike many of Costa Rica's other volcanoes, the mythology surrounding Barva doesn't tell the story of the volcano's fiery formation. Instead, it tells the tale of the lake, Laguna de Barva, and how it came to be. The story of Laguna de Barva is one of Costa Rica's oldest ghost stories, centered around the dangers of breaking a promise and acting based on greed.

The story begins with two Spanish conquistadors, who were lost in the mountains around Barva. While they desperately searched for the path home, they instead stumbled upon a treasure - piles and piles of gold that had been mysteriously abandoned in the forest. The two men were overcome by greed and tried desperately to take the gold with them, although it would make their journey much more difficult and they had not eaten in days. With the effort of carrying the gold, one of the men fell ill, weak from starvation. He knew that he could not take a single step more, and decided that he would lie down where he stood. The dying man implored his traveling partner to continue without him and made the other man promise that he would use the gold to build a church once he found civilization. As he emotionally bid his friend farewell, the remaining man promised that he would.

The remaining conquistador continued his journey alone, and gradually, the isolation and hunger made his mind turn to greed. He could think of many better things to use the gold for, instead of building a church - and as he was sure that his traveling companion had now passed away, he felt sure that he could break the promise. That night, the man fell asleep - and was shocked to wake up next to the corpse of his friend, as if he had never continued the journey at all. He sat up and looked around, noticing the sound of sobbing from nearby.

The sobbing came from a young woman, who was perched on a rock nearby. Still terrified, and half-convinced that he was hallucinating, the conquistador asked the woman what was wrong. She replied that she was crying because of the broken promise, and no matter how much the man tried to comfort her, she continued to weep. Despite his promises that he would use the gold to build a church as promised, the weeping woman did not believe him – she could see the greed in his heart and knew that he would break his promise. Eventually, the man gave up on consoling her, and went on to leave. He turned back and asked her name.

The woman replied that her name was "Pilar" – the early version of the Virgin Mary herself. It was Pilar's tears that flowed to the ground, gradually creating a body of water that would become known as the Laguna de Barva. This is where the story ends, and nobody knows what happened to the surviving conquistador, or if he ever decided to keep the promise to his dying friend.

With such a moving origin story, it's no wonder that many find the Laguna de Barva to be a deeply moving and slightly eerie sight. Surrounded by constantly shifting fog and low-hanging clouds, the lake is a place where it is easy to get lost in quiet thought. Some locals believe that if you spend enough time by the shores of Laguna de Barva, you may be lucky enough to see the faint outline of a ghostly church or a weeping woman, floating just above the surface of the lake.

EL PUENTA DE PIERDA

A Deal with the Devil

Near Grecia, an understated attraction lies in the form of an ancient stone bridge, named Puente de Piedra, around a fifteen-minute bus trip away from the main town. According to local legend, this is a one-of-a-kind bridge, with the nearest possible replica being as far away as China.

Following the short trail to the bridge on foot will allow you to appreciate the architecture up close, and enjoy observing the flight of the flocks of swallows that make their home under the bridge. El Puente de Piedra is a favorite location for a picnic, away from the hustle and bustle of the Town Centre. While the stone bridge is relatively small, the tale of its origin is anything but unimpressive. In fact, locals still insist that the bridge was built by the Devil himself.

Legend has it that a Costa Rican farmer desperately needed to cross the river, but he had no way to do so. In his despair, he called out to the Devil and promised that the Devil could have his soul as payment for constructing a bridge over the river. However, the clever farmer added a clause to his promise - the Devil could only take his soul if construction of the bridge was successfully completed by the time the rooster crowed the following morning. Thinking that this was an easy bargain, the Devil readily agreed and looked forward to dragging the farmer's soul back down to hell.

The local farmer watched as the Devil began to work in the hot sun, fishing out large stones from the river and slotting them together to form the shape of the bridge we see today. As the bridge began to take form, the farmer observed carefully, until finally, there was only one small hole left to fill with stone before the bridge was completed. Before the Devil could add the final stone, the farmer grabbed a nearby rooster and pulled firmly on the bird's tail. Startled, the rooster began to crow. The farmer had cleverly deceived the devil, and was able to escape with both the bridge and his own soul.

The bridge's missing stone is the subject of one of the highlights of visiting this location: peering at the bridge from above, putting oneself in the footsteps of the clever farmer, and trying to see the hole where the final piece of stone should have been laid. While the missing stone might be due to erosion over time or a lazy builder in ancient times, there is no proof either way - and it's more fun to imagine the clever farmer, tugging on the rooster's tail and saving his own soul in exchange for a bridge with a single missing stone.

BASILICA OF OUR LADY OF THE ANGELS

A Traveling Statue

Cartago's Basilica of Our Lady of the Angels is one of Costa Rica's most sacred sites of worship. The church rises above its surroundings, with towering pillars and ornate golden domes. At night, illuminated from the outside by soft lighting, it becomes even more stunning. However, the main attraction of the Basilica of Our Lady of the Angels is not the church itself, but a small and understated stone statue that lies within its walls.

Basilica of Our Lady of the Angels is a common site for Costa Ricans to journey to on a religious pilgrimage, a dedicated walk of 22 kilometers from San José, which ends with arrival at a very special rock inside the basilica. The local name for this pilgrimage is Romería, and it remains one of the most popular pilgrimage journeys in the modern day. During Romería, this sacred rock is visited both upon arrival, and regularly during each pilgrim's stay at the church to wash themselves and drink water from the rock. But in such a beautiful, historical basilica, why is there such a focus on a rock?

The legend behind the rock within the Basilica of Our Lady of the Angels, like so many Costa Rican tales, begins with a young and curious girl. The girl was exploring near the site where the church would one day be constructed when she saw a small object sitting on a rock. When she came closer, she discovered that it was a delicately carved statue made of dark, shiny stone. It depicted the Virgin Mary, with a gentle expression on her face, holding the baby Jesus in her arms. The girl tucked the statue into her pocket and decided to keep it.

However, when she woke up the next morning, she couldn't find the statue anywhere. Determined not to lose her precious treasure, the girl found her way back to the rock where she had first found the statue - and was shocked to find that the little stone lady was sitting on the rock again as if she had never left. Scared by the statue's unexplained movement, the girl picked up the statue and hurried to take it to the local priest. In response, the priest decided to lock the statue away in a box, so that it could not worry the girl by moving again. The next morning, the box was empty…and once again, the stone statue was back on the rock.

During this time, the construction of the church that would become the Basilica of Our Lady of the Angels was underway, but the location of the building was slightly different from what it is today. Each time progress was made with construction, an earthquake would rumble through the town, and the church would be destroyed. All this time, the statue kept reappearing on the rock. Finally, the decision was made to change the site where the church was being constructed. Many of the people involved believed that it was no coincidence that the Virgin Mary statue kept reappearing on the same rock, while the church was repeatedly destroyed by nature. Perhaps, this was a sign that they must build the basilica in the location where the statue had appeared.

Sure enough, as soon as the basilica was moved to the new site, its construction was able to be completed without interference from earthquakes. Today, the same statue is kept in the heart of the basilica, safe within a beautiful golden shell. Some people refer to her as Reina de Cartago (Queen of Cartago), as she has been crowned as Costa Rica's official patron, or La Negrita, due to the dark color of the stone she is carved from.

Whether the statue was truly displeased at the original site of the construction of the basilica, or the new location was simply on more stable ground, one thing is for certain: this origin story inspires faith and awe across Costa Rica. With this backstory behind the statue, it is unsurprising that La Negrita and the Basilica of Our Lady of the Angels remain such objects of reverence even in the modern day. While the 22-kilometer pilgrimage from San José is the most common, worshippers will journey to visit the Basilica of Our Lady of the Angels from many different locations throughout Costa Rica. The most devout of the pilgrims will choose to showcase their devotion by traveling the final leg of their journey by crawling on the ground towards the basilica.

An interesting part of this pilgrimage is that, although the water from the rock where La Negrita was found is not chemically treated or purified in any way, it appears completely safe to drink. None of the pilgrims who have drunk the water or washed themselves in it have gotten sick, and scientific analysis of the water itself showed that it was astonishingly clean and fresh despite not being filtered. There is no scientific explanation for this phenomenon - it truly is a modern miracle.

The Basilica of Our Lady of the Angels is open for visitors all year round, and anybody is welcome to enter the basilica for prayer, observation, or paying respects to Reina de Cartago at any time. Some visitors choose to bring silver medals in the shape of different body parts, representing an area of the body that may be in ill health. By leaving these silver representations in front of the statue, many believers hope that La Negrita will bless them with a cure. If you are interested to see these unique medals as a physical representation of faith, a selection of older medals can be viewed in the museum by the basilica.

SANTIAGO APÓSTOL PARISH RUINS

The Dangers of Jealousy

The ruins of Santiago Apóstol Parish are a tourist location with a rich history, tormented by a natural disaster. Set in the heart of Cartago, the ruins have been transformed over time into a lush green garden, offering a range of flowering plants and places to sit and enjoy the scenery. With elegant topiary, ponds, and original architecture, both tourists and locals alike find the ruins of Santiago Apóstol Parish to be a favorite site for relaxation and appreciation of nature.

While referred to as "ruins", the remaining elements of the church are technically not ruins at all - as the church was never successfully built in the first place, the "ruins" are more of an abandoned building project than anything else. This site has been the home of several different churches since the first church was opened in 1575 - but none of the churches in this particular location have been able to stand for long! The first church was destroyed in 1630 by an earthquake, and the replacement chapels were damaged by a second earthquake in 1718...and then finally, the church was toppled by the San Antolín earthquake in 1841.

The determined local people made one final attempt to rebuild in 1870, using a visually striking Romanesque style, but this rebuild was never completed due to yet another earthquake in 1910. Since 1910, there have been no further attempts to rebuild. The ruins have been allowed to be what they are - stark, visually striking reminders of the power of nature, and the relics of a building from another time.

With the Santiago Apóstol Parish's unfortunate luck with earthquakes, it's no wonder that local folklore attempts to explain why the churches were unable to remain standing. The legend behind the parish tells the story of two of Cartago's early settlers, who were a pair of brothers. The first brother was a popular, handsome man, while the other was a reserved priest. Both of the brothers fell in love, but unfortunately, their hearts were stolen by the same woman. Overlooking the priest, the woman fell in love with the popular brother. Overcome with envy and filled with the fire of heartbreak, the priest lashed out and confronted his brother in the church one night. In his rage, the priest fatally stabbed his brother. Immediately, he was full of regret - but it was too late. In repentance for his crime, the priest set out to build a church, as an apology to God and his brother for the life that he had taken within the sacred walls of the church.

Only a year after the priest had constructed the church to atone for his crime, the building was destroyed by an earthquake. This pattern repeated, with new churches being built, and new earthquakes turning them to rubble. Many locals believe that the priest's crime, and the tragic death of his brother at his hand, have led to the church being cursed to be destroyed by earthquakes whenever it is rebuilt. The more superstitious locals report that, on particularly dark and misty nights, the ghost of the priest can be seen. He wanders through the Santiago Apóstol Parish ruins, unable to rest in peace due to his sins.

With the rich history underlying the ruins, the fact that construction was abandoned and replaced with a peaceful, flourishing garden lends the story a kind of poetic justice. In fact, sitting in the gardens and observing the flow of visitors, singing birds, and native plants inspires a feeling of worship and appreciation very similar to what one might find in the pew of a church.

POAS VOLCANO

How the Rualdo Bird Lost Its Song

With the largest active volcanic crater in the world, the Poas Volcano is truly a sight to be seen. In the hiking trails through Poas Volcano National Park, you can see the awe-inspiring sight of the volcano's acidic lake, bubbling with clouds of rising steam. From time to time, the volcano will give her observers a real show, by shooting geysers of steam up to 250 meters in the air. The surrounding cloud forest, full of thriving nature and low-hanging mist, is just as awe-inspiring as the volcano itself.

Despite Poas Volcano's explosive and intense appearance, the mythology surrounding the area is surprisingly soft and sweet. In fact, the Poas Volcano is the site of one of Costa Rica's most popular fables; the story of the Rualdo bird. Often referred to as "how the Rualdo bird lost its song", this is a sad but beautiful story that only adds to the beauty of the Poas Volcano and its surroundings.

The story begins with a young girl, who belonged to a tribe that lived near the Poas Volcano. One day, while the girl was playing in the rainforest, she came across a beautiful bright green and yellow bird - the Rualdo bird. The girl was delighted at the beauty of the bird's plumage, and the sound of its melodic, cheerful song. She was kind to the bird, offering it friendship, and the bird trusted her not to harm him. From that day forward, the bird came with the girl wherever she went, and the unlikely pair were the best of friends.

However, this happiness could not last forever, as the girl's tribe was troubled by the Poas Volcano. The young girl's father was one of the tribe's shamans, and he had become increasingly worried about the explosive eruptions of the nearby Poas Volcano. He believed that, in a fit of rage, the volcano would erupt and cover the tribe's village with lava and volcanic ash. Finally, he could not live in fear any longer. As he was one of the most powerful shamans in the tribe, he felt that it was his responsibility to fix this issue. The girl's father made the journey to the very top of the volcano so that he might speak with the spirit of the volcano itself.

When the shaman asked the volcano what he could do to calm its anger, the answer made his very heart sink into his chest and filled him with despair. The volcano's spirit answered that there was only one sacrifice that would appease it and quell its anger: the life of the shaman's cherished daughter. Although the shaman loved his daughter very much, his fear of the Poas Volcano was so great that he agreed to pay the price in order to ensure the safety of the rest of his village. When the shaman returned home to the village, he gave the orders for his daughter to be carried to the summit of the volcano, at any cost.

The girl was quickly captured by the other villages, who carried her all the way to the volcano's summit. Throughout the journey, she cried and screamed, kicked and struggled, but it was no good - she could not escape. Unseen by the others, the Rualdo bird followed behind, full of anguish at the plight of his best friend.

Her captors prepared to throw the girl into the volcano's fiery crater, when a flash of bright green flew through the air. The Rualdo bird soared ahead of the girl, plummeting into the volcano's crater and singing out as loud as he could. In his song, he begged the spirit of the volcano to have mercy and spare the girl's life. The volcano was touched by the show of friendship, and agreed to spare the life of the young girl - but only in exchange for the voice of the Rualdo bird. From this moment forward, the Rualdo bird's voice vanished forevermore.

In response to the Rualdo bird's final song, the Poas Volcano was full of emotion and began to weep deeply as its anger was replaced by sadness. As the volcano's tears flowed and flowed, they began to fill one of the craters with clear, mineral-rich water. Today, that same crater lake is named the Botos Lagoon...and it has been inactive since that day.

The little green bird, called the Rualdo, still exists in Costa Rica today - if you visit Poas Volcano, you may even be lucky enough to spot one! However, just like the legend states, you will be unlikely to hear its call. The only noise the Rualdo bird can make is a soft whistling noise. But perhaps the little bird's sacrifice was not in vain: the crater that became the Botos Lagoon has not erupted in thousands of years and is now full of beautifully clear water and surrounded by pristine cloud forest.

If you wish to see the site where the Rualdo bird lost his voice, Poas Volcano's multiple trails and observation points offer views of both the peaceful Botos Lagoon, the two inactive craters, and the explosive activity of the main crater. Poas Volcano is truly a site where the gentleness and violence of nature can be clearly observed, side-by-side, and acting in harmony with one another.

LOS QUETZALES NATIONAL PARK

Divine Protection

L os Quetzales National Park, set high in Costa Rica's impressive Talamanca mountains, gives tourists and locals alike the opportunity to enter into another world. Surrounded by the thick clouds that linger at high altitudes, the National Park's cloud forest is a piece of nature that is undisturbed by the hustle and bustle of the city. Los Quetzales National Park can be accessed from San Gerardo de Dota, where there is a ranger station that's easily accessible.

Visitors to Los Quetzales National Park will see an array of flora and fauna, from rare Costa Rican alpine plants to exotic wild animals such as deer, tapirs, jaguars, and monkeys. Even the foliage and low-hanging thick mist of the cloud forest alone is enough reason for a visit. However, there's one particular animal sighting that most visitors hope for even more than the rest - the chance to catch a glimpse of a Resplendent quetzal. The Resplendent quetzal is the National Park's namesake for good reason, as this is one of the best locations in Costa Rica to guarantee a sighting of this shy creature.

The Resplendent quetzal, a small bird with glittering green feathers and an elegantly flowing long tail, is so elegant that it almost appears otherworldly. With a soft song, and striking patterns of crimson feathers contrasting with the green, the Resplendent quetzal has captured the hearts and imaginations of many. It's no surprise that Costa Rican mythology depicts the quetzal as truly being a bridge between the spiritual and the divine, by acting as a messenger from the spirits themselves.

In both the Bribrí and Boruca indigenous tribes of Costa Rica, mythology includes a strong belief that the spirits of the deceased - or of the Gods - can be housed within the bodies of specific animals on Earth. The animals can act as a messenger for the spirit that they carry, or provide protection to others that the spirit holds dear. Boruca folklore believes that the quetzal, in particular, carried the spirit of one great historical figure - a legendary Boruca warrior by the name of Satú.

Satú's birth was hailed by the soft song of a Resplendent quetzal, who alighted in the center of the village and sang out loud to the rest of the village on the day that the great warrior would be born. Upon hearing such a song from a shy and quiet bird, Satú's tribe decided to make a quetzal-shaped medallion for the newborn baby, to offer him divine protection and bring him luck. As Satú grew, he quickly became a strong and ferocious warrior. As long as the quetzal medallion was hanging around his neck, he was never wounded in battle, and his success only continued to grow as he became older, wiser, and stronger.

But not everybody was happy about Satú's success. Born as the son of a legendary chief, and given the protection of the quetzal from birth, some of the others in the tribe began to feel jealous of Satú. The most jealous of all was the warrior's uncle, who finally couldn't stand it any longer. While Satú was sleeping, his uncle snuck beside him and slipped the medallion free from his neck, leaving him unprotected when he woke in the morning. Although Satú searched and searched, his medallion was nowhere to be found. That day, Satú's uncle murdered his nephew in a fit of jealousy, and without the protection of the quetzal medallion, the great warrior Satú succumbed to his wounds.

As Satú took his last breath, a Resplendent quetzal appeared in the surrounding forest and flew to Satú's body. As the quetzal flew away, the bird carried the spirit of the great warrior Satú with it, taking Satú to live in the cloud forest in the mountains forevermore.

Los Quetzales National Park is one of the most common places in Costa Rica to catch sight of a Resplendent quetzal, but you'll need to look carefully - the green of the quetzal's feathers allows them to blend seamlessly in with the forest around them. In the dense cloud cover of the national park, they can be almost invisible on a foggy day.

But when you are fortunate enough to see the ethereal presence of a quetzal in person, it's easy to see why they were given their role in Costa Rican mythology. From the iridescent green feathers to the tail that trails behind them as they fly, the Resplendent quetzal is truly a sight to behold. Just as the legend says, the song of the quetzal is breathtaking, with a melody of soft notes drifting through the trees.

MONTEVERDE CLOUD FOREST RESERVE

A Hunted God

With a name that translates to "Green Mountain", Monteverde Cloud Forest Reserve is an oasis of vibrant cloud forest that was voted as one of Costa Rica's seven wonders. The winding walkways constructed in the cloud forest canopy of the reserve provide a vantage point to see the lush forest from a bird's eye view, and the option for zip-lining through the tree line is available for more adventurous explorers. The Cloud Forest's elevated walkways were created by ecologists looking to study the vast array of wildlife in the area, and remain today as a way for visitors to truly experience the wonders of Monteverde Cloud Forest Reserve.

One of the wildlife highlights of Monteverde Cloud Forest Reserve is the chance to spy on one of Costa Rica's most revered and elusive animals - the tapir. The tapir is a prominent figure in the folklore of Costa Rica's indigenous Bribrí people, and they are still cherished and protected today. The mythology surrounding the tapir proposes that every tapir in the world carries the same spirit - the spirit of Tapir, a God also known by the name Nãmãitãmĩ.

Legend has it that as Tapir's brother, the God named Sibú, was creating the world, he successfully created a beautiful blue sky - but the planet he created was nothing more than dry rock, where animals and plants could not live. After hearing that his sister Tapir had given birth to a child, named Iriria, Sibú wondered if Tapir's baby would be able to become the Earth. He sent a messenger in the form of a vampire bat to bite Iriria. The vampire bat returned to Sibú, and soon after drinking Iriria's blood, the bat's droppings began to bloom into sprawling vines and green plants. This is how the Earth became covered in green grass and trees, and in the Monteverde Cloud Forest, you are surrounded by evidence of how Tapir's baby gave life to the world.

But this is not the only story connecting Tapir to modern Costa Rica, and to the Bribrí. A second piece of folklore tells the tale of Sibú plotting to find a wife of his own in exchange for marrying off his unwilling sister Tapir. However, Tapir was able to look into the future and knew of Sibú's plan to betray her by sending her into an unhappy marriage. When she told her brother that she would not agree to marry, Sibú retaliated by transferring some of Tapir's spirit down to the mortal realm so that she could be hunted by the Bribrí - while appearing as a humble tapir.

This origin story has connections to modern-day Costa Rican traditions, merging legend with reality. Bribrí culture has firm restrictions about how and when tapir can be hunted, out of respect for Tapir and her punishment. In every Bribrí village, one woman is selected to become the only villager who is properly trained to prepare and cook a tapir. As well as this, tapir hunting is surrounded by ceremony, and only some groups of the Bribrí are permitted to hunt the tapir. These ceremonies are not just out of respect - the Bribrí believe that violating these terms will anger Tapir and cause her to seek revenge on those who have wronged her.

While tapirs are Costa Rica's largest land mammal, they are shy, solitary and tend to avoid humans. Looking at a tapir, it's hard to believe that these gentle creatures could contain part of the spirit of one of the Gods - but with their elusive nature, one can imagine Tapir trying to stay quiet and hide from those who wish to hunt her. Because tapirs are nocturnal, your best chance of spotting one in the wild is visiting Monteverde Cloud Forest Reserve near dawn or dusk - although sometimes, an elusive tapir can be sighted during the day.

If you don't see a tapir at Monteverde Cloud Forest Reserve, there are many other natural wonders to fill your visit – the Resplendent quetzal is found here, as well as other native Costa Rican animals such as monkeys, jaguars, and sloths.

THE RIO TELIRE

A Tale of Justice

Río Telire is an impressive, rugged river that flows through Costa Rica's Talamanca Mountains and toward the Caribbean. Off the beaten path, the river can be seen via a boat trip with a local guide. Because of the isolated location of the Río Telire, indigenous groups are able to thrive away from intrusion, inhabiting the protected land, farming the cacao plant to make chocolate, and raising crops. The two prominent indigenous tribes in the area are the Bribri tribe and the Cabécar tribe.

Touring of the Río Telire isn't just visually rich, with sights of dense forest, native animals, and the roaring rapids of the river itself - it is also a culturally rich experience, where local guides can share knowledge and the folklore behind the region itself. It is an opportunity to step away from the more common tourist spots and truly learn about the history that weaves together to make Costa Rica what it is today. Given the rugged terrain of the area surrounding Río Telire, the river gained a role in indigenous mythology as a very special hiding spot for one particular character.

In Bribri and Cabécar folklore, the "hurricane children" are the offspring of the first family that stepped foot on planet Earth - the thunder family. The hurricane children were chaotic, playful, and loud, running in circles to create gale-force winds, and setting hurricanes and thunderstorms upon the land instead of staying home with their mother. One day, on their adventures around the world, the hurricane children met their uncle, the Sun Lord. He advised them that they should return home, and play calmly, instead of creating chaos with their games. The children followed the Sun Lord's advice, but when they arrived home, their mother was gone - and in her place, there was a pile of bones.

The hurricane children heard a ghostly voice coming from the bones, and realized that they stood in front of their mother's skeleton. In the mother's last words to her children, she told them that she was overjoyed to have them home and that her only wish was that they would be obedient and respectful in the future. Devastated at the loss of their mother, the children asked how she had died. Their mother responded that she had been murdered by the Lady of the Mountain, who went by the name Sakabiali. Sakabiali had caused her death by forcing her to chase a deer through the mountains and forests, day and night, until Sakabiali ambushed the exhausted woman in a tiny passageway. Then, Sakabialia had drained her body of blood, and eaten what remained, leaving only a skeleton behind.

Determined to avenge their mother's death, the hurricane children set out to find Sakabiali and make her answer for the crime she had committed. After searching high and low, they discovered her hiding place - in Talamanca, by the Río Telire. Thrilled by their success, the hurricane children decided to stop and play for a while. As they played, one of the siblings remembered an important piece of information - the Lady of the Mountain, Sakabiali, had a love for eating spicy peppers. Finding a chili pepper growing nearby, the children used it as bait to lure Sakabiali from her hiding place.

Realizing that she was trapped, Sakabiali told the children the reason she had murdered their mother. She had been starving, and felt alone, as nobody took care of her. The devious hurricane children asked Sakabiali for one favor: to reenact what she had done to cause their mother's death. Sakabiali fell for the children's trick, and the hurricane children killed the Lady of the Mountain just as she had killed their mother.

With their revenge exacted, the hurricane children returned to visit Lord Sun, telling their uncle of their mother's death and what they had done to avenge her. Instead of praising the children, Lord Sun was displeased. He asked the children to avoid destruction and revenge, and instead practice living in harmony together as a family.

While Costa Rica's thunderstorms suggest that the hurricane children might still be playing today, visiting the pristine area surrounding the Río Telire makes it easy to see how Sakabiali could have remained hidden in the dense native forest, protected by the rushing rapids of the Río Telire. In the modern day, the best part about visiting Río Telire is learning about the history of the area from those who know best - the people who have lived there for centuries, surrounded by Costa Rica's wilderness.

SANATORIO DURÁN

Haunted Story

For those who love ghost stories, Costa Rica offers nothing better than the country's most haunted location - the Sanatorio Durán, or the Duran Sanatorium. Located near Cartago, a thirty-minute drive from San Jose, the Sanatorio Durán is tucked away in the mountainous scenery, with a backdrop of rolling fields of seasonal farmland and the looming Irazú Volcano nearby. Looking at it from the outside, it's hard to imagine why the Sanitorium gained its haunted reputation - but as Sanatorio Durán is open to the public, curious minds can wander throughout the grounds and answer this question for themselves.

Sanatorio Durán's story didn't begin with ghosts, instead, the building was originally created in the early 1900s as a source of hope. Built by a doctor, after whom the Sanitorium is named, it was created as an isolated hospital where patients with tuberculosis could be safely treated without risking spreading the disease to others. The beautiful location of the hospital, which is still breathtaking today, was thought to help patients to heal by immersing them in nature and outdoor scenery. Some believe that the doctor's motivation for building such an extensive hospital was more personal than that, as his young daughter is rumored to have been sick with tuberculosis at the time the hospital was built.

The Sanatorio Durán housed both patients with tuberculosis and patients who had a variety of mental health issues causing them to require hospitalization. With hundreds of patients able to live in the sprawling Sanitorium at a time, the nuns who helped to treat them were kept busy. When tuberculosis became a thing of the past, the Sanatorio Durán was converted to other uses - it spent some time functioning as an orphanage, and then as a prison. Eventually, due to damage from the volatile Irazú volcano, the building was damaged irreparably and shut its doors for good.

Now, the buildings of the once-magnificent hospital are crumbling and covered with graffiti, but every room and building that makes up the Sanitorium is still rich with history.

It's easy to imagine the thousands of people who have lived and died within its walls, and easier still to see how the sloping scenery would be healing.

Many visitors to the Sanatorio Durán report that they get shivers down their spine and feel uneasy from the moment they step foot on the grounds. There are rumors that fully-charged electronics will inexplicably go flat when inside the Sanatorio Durán, or that electronics will not work the way that they should. People often experience a strange cold draft when exploring the abandoned buildings of the Sanitorium, even when there is no obvious source for the breeze. However, these strange happenings aren't the spookiest thing to occur at the Sanatorio Durán, with many visitors insisting that they have seen a spirit, or apparition, wandering the grounds.

The most commonly sighted ghost at the Sanatorio Durán is suspected to be none other than the daughter of the doctor who opened the hospital, who is widely believed to have died of tuberculosis despite her loving father's best efforts. Most reports of the young girl's ghost are seen in the Sanatorio Durán's chapel, where she perches on the roof looking out at the grounds.

Another apparition that is commonly reported is that of a

nun, who would have worked tirelessly in the hospital treating patients during her life. A common thread in sightings of the nun is that visitors felt that she was not violent or malicious, but instead, she was unable to leave the boundaries of the hospital due to her mission to continue helping the sick and mentally ill, even in death.

This history provides the perfect storm for a haunting - a tragic beginning with a critically ill daughter, and the flood of mentally ill patients, orphans, and prisoners who came in and out of the Sanitorium's doors. Whether or not it is truly haunted is something that you will have to decide for yourself after exploring the grounds of the old hospital. But even if there are no ghosts to be seen, the history embedded in every part of the hospital's grounds, as well as the stunning scenery that was thought to be healing for every patient who walked through the doors, are enough of a reward.

THE STONE SPHERES

Weapons of the Gods

I n every country, there is a part of history that cannot be explained - an unresolved mystery that tourists and locals alike will ponder for hundreds of years to come. One of Costa Rica's biggest mysteries is the hundreds of ancient stone spheres, or "bolas de piedra" (stone balls) which can be found on Isla de Caño and the Diquís Delta. They are sometimes called the Diquís spheres because many believe that they were created by the pre-Columbian Diquís people as long ago as 400 AD.

The sites where the stone spheres were found often included burial sites and paved areas, as well as other artifacts which vary from site to site. Most of the stone spheres have now been moved from the locations where they were originally found, but a collection of the spheres can be viewed in San Jose at Costa Rica's National Museum, or in many other locations around Costa Rica - some smaller spheres are even used as lawn ornaments!

If you would prefer to see the stone spheres in a more natural environment, the Museum of the Stone Spheres at the UNESCO World Heritage Site Finca 6, is the best place to view the spheres in their original location. Not only can you view the spheres in their placement, the Museum of the Stone Spheres is full of rich history, allowing visitors to absorb the culture of the area and surround themselves with ancient mythology and history.

The real origin of the stone spheres will remain a mystery, but archaeologists have several theories about how they came to be, and why and how they were used. A popular theory is that the stone spheres were selectively placed on the paths that led to the houses of important people in the village, such as chiefs - but nobody knows why the spheres were so important, or why so much effort went into making them. Some believe that the size of the spheres was used to communicate the power of the chief and that perhaps more powerful members of the community would have larger spheres by their houses.

As for the perfectly round shape of the spheres, some archaeologists believe that the people who made the spheres were inspired by the moon and stars above, or that the arrangement of the spheres was even used to represent the layout of our solar system. Possibly, the original arrangement of the spheres could give some insight into the astronomy knowledge of this ancient culture - but as most of the spheres have been moved, this knowledge is lost for good.

But the theories as to the origin of the stone spheres, like so many pieces of Costa Rican history, move away from the physical world and into the world of the Gods. Like any mysterious wonder of the world, there are many pieces of local folklore that theorize about how the stones came to be, and what they were designed for in the first place. The indigenous Bribri people of Costa Rica believe that the spheres were an ancient weapon of the Gods themselves, used by Tara, the God of thunder. When Tara was fighting against the Gods of wind, the Serkes, he used an unusual weapon to chase them away - an enormous blowpipe, which he filled with gigantic stone balls. The balls that he shot at the Serkes landed on the ground, discarded, and remain there today as the stone spheres - which the Bribri call "Tara's cannonballs".

While the spheres are certainly large enough to have been

used as Tara's cannonballs, with some of them more than 6 feet in diameter and weighing as much as 15 tons, in reality, their perfect cannonball shape may not have always been the case. The perfect roundness of the spheres has always mystified visitors, but due to exposure to the elements and erosion over the centuries, it is impossible to know the size and shape of the original spheres. Archaeologists believe that the spheres, which are made from a type of rock called gabbro, were made by hammering large rocks into a rounder shape and then smoothed into perfect roundness with abrasive sand.

If you are interested in unresolved mysteries, there is no better way to ponder the creation of Costa Rica's stone spheres than by going to see them in person. Whether they were created by nature, man, or the God of thunder himself, they are a majestic and awe-inspiring sight.

CLUB SPORT CARTAGINÉS

A Tale of Two Curses

To truly experience the vibrance and joy of Costa Rica, there is one attraction that cannot be missed: watching a game of football. Football is Costa Rica's most popular sport, and the country goes wild supporting their favorite team and celebrating wins, especially in the national championships. But in Costa Rica, football is much more than just a game. It is a source of unity and community, a source of pride, and a way to connect with others despite differences.

If you want to view a football game in Costa Rica, look no further than La Sabana in San Jose – the world-class stadium that is the country's love letter to the sport of football. Viewing a football game at La Sabana Stadium is one of the many ways anyone can immerse themselves into the heart of Costa Rican culture for a few hours, and truly experience the love that Costa Ricans have for football. The chanting, the waving, the cheering, and the enthusiastic crowds dressed in team colors - there is no better experience for a visitor to Costa Rica.

However, there is one Costa Rican football team whose fans are never able to celebrate after the championships. As the Premier Division's oldest football team, it may seem surprising that Club Sport Cartaginés were burdened with an unbroken losing streak in the national championships. Beginning in 1941, it seemed that bad luck followed the team - but many Costa Ricans believe that there is much more to it than that. In fact, rumor has it that Club Sport Cartaginés were cursed, preventing them from achieving success.

Supposedly, the curse began in 1940, when the Club Sport Cartaginés had just won the championship and went out to celebrate in Cartago. In celebration, the team grew rowdy and disrespectful and rode their horses into the Basilica of Our Lady of the Angeles. The Basilica's priest was irate at their disrespect, and ordered the team to leave immediately - but not before he placed a curse on them as punishment for their behavior. From that day forward, the Club Sport Cartaginés were unable to win another championship, so they were unable to repeat the rowdy celebrations that had cursed them to begin with!

For such a lengthy stretch of unlikely bad luck, it makes sense that the Club Sport Cartaginés is rumored to have been the victim of another curse, which began around the same time. This curse, however, was not set upon the team by a furious priest, but by El Muñeco - a small "voodoo doll" which was secretly buried in the soil under the football team's home turf. Nobody knows who the curse was placed by, only that whoever buried the doll was determined to prevent the team from succeeding. Believers in the curse of El Muñeco alleged that, unless the doll was uncovered and removed from the Fello Meza stadium, the curse could not be broken.

However, it seems like the team's luck has changed. In the 2021-2022 season, Club Sport Cartaginés were finally able to bring home the national title after defeating Liga Deportiva Alajuelense. Perhaps the priest's curse has finally worn off…or maybe a particularly superstitious fan was able to locate the site where El Muñeco was buried. Whatever the case may be, one thing's for sure: Club Sport Cartaginés' bad luck has finally run out.

If you choose to view a game at La Sabana Stadium, it's easy to spend the day there - in fact, the La Sabana Metropolitan

Park next to the stadium offers a range of outdoor activities. From the stunning lake, to the sprawling trails for jogging and walking, it's not far from the chaos of a football game to the serene peace of Costa Rican nature. Just make sure that, no matter how hard you celebrate, you avoid riding on horseback into any of the area's churches.

RINCÓN DE LA VIEJA (THE OLD WOMAN'S CORNER)

Tragedy and Redemption

There is no better place in Costa Rica to be amazed by the brutal power of nature than Rincón de la Vieja National Park. Found in Guanacaste, this volcanic national park offers views of steaming pits of boiling mud, mineral water vents, and both the Rincón de la Vieja and Santa Maria volcanoes.

Despite the impressive boiling water vents and mineral pools that bubble restlessly, there is a peaceful element to the surrounding forest within the Rincón de la Vieja National Park. Visitors can see a wide array of Costa Rican animals, from the shy tapir to big cats such as jaguars stalking through the brush. The park is one of the rare locations in the country where the white morpho butterfly breeds and lucky visitors during the rainy season might catch a glimpse of the unique, pearlescent wings fluttering through the trees. For tourists and botany lovers, Rincón de la Vieja is also the best place in Costa Rica to see the guaria morada orchid - the national flower of the country, which fills the park with purple blooms in spring.

Visitors to the Rincón de la Vieja National Park might wonder about the name of the park, which translates to "Old Woman's Corner". The "old woman" that the volcano and the park itself are named after is supposedly the spirit of a woman named Curubandá, who has lived within the Rincón de la Vieja volcano since ancient times.

Curubandá was an indigenous healer in the area, but she could not follow the traditions of her tribe. She craved love more than anything else, and yet none of the men in her own tribe had stolen her heart. Instead, she looked elsewhere - and soon, she fell in love with the leader of a rival tribe, named Mixcoac. Curubandá's father found out about the love his daughter had for Mixcoac, who was his sworn enemy. In his rage, he decided that the only solution was to murder his daughter's lover, by throwing the man into the pit of an active volcano.

However, there was something that Curubandá's father did

not know - his daughter and Mixcoac had conceived a child together, and Curubandá had become pregnant. Desperate to keep her pregnancy a secret from her father and the rest of the tribe, Curubandá snuck away from the village and made her way to the summit of the volcano, so that she could give birth in secret. The looming forest and steep climb made her confident that she would not be found. In her grief, Curubandá made a painful decision once her baby was born - she believed that her newborn child should join Mixcoac, and so she picked up the baby and threw it into the volcano's maw.

Heavy with grief and guilt, Curubandá could not return to her village, where she would have to look her father in the eye knowing the pain he had brought upon her. Instead, in the thick forest surrounding the volcano, Curubandá decided to spend the rest of her days in secrecy. She began helping travelers with wounds or illnesses, taking on a role as a healer that helped to alleviate her guilt for what she had done to her child. Word began to spread about this aging healer who lived in the forest, and when travelers announced that they were going to see the healer, they said they were going "al rincón de la vieja" - "to the old woman's corner".

Some versions of this story are less violent, believing that Curubandá's children and their father fell victim to an eruption of the volcano, or fell in the crater during a journey to the summit. But all versions of the myth have one thing in common: Curubandá went through a terrible tragedy and was unable to move on with her life. Through it all, she made every effort to help others, whether this was by warning them of the dangers of the active volcano, or by providing healing treatments to strangers who had become lost in the mountains.

Many believe that the spirit of Curubandá never moved on from the volcano even in death, and that the ghost of the healer still walks the mountain paths in Rincón de la Vieja National Park. Most of the reported sightings of the ghost of the old woman are near Santa Maria's crater, where she is believed to warn travelers of the dangers of the active volcano and even help lost tourists find their way back to the path.

If a spirit is warning tourists away from the active volcanic crater of Santa Maria, it's for the best - the volcano is very active, with frequent eruptions of flowing mud and debris. But visitors can rest assured that even if they do see the spirit, by all accounts, she is a benevolent and kind woman who just wants to help others.

Like so many of Costa Rica's natural wonders, Rincón de la Vieja National Park is a place where the tragedy of mythology, the violence of nature, and the beauty of Mother Earth meet. The National Park contains more than thirty rivers and smaller creeks, and tourists wanting a break from volcanic viewing can hike to view the world-renowned Cangreja waterfall rushing into the blue lagoon at its base. Whether you are interested in the tragic folklore, flora and fauna, or simply the sights of the active volcanoes, Rincón de la Vieja National Park is not to be missed.

RIO AGUA CALIENTE, CARTAGO

The Fountain of Youth

I n Cartago, Costa Rica, there is a hot spring that has been
sought by visitors and locals alike for many centuries.
Located on Cartago's outskirts, the Pura Pora hot springs, or
the Rio Agua Caliente Cartago, have secured a spot as one of
the most famous natural hot springs in the world - but this
miraculous body of water was almost lost to history.

The powers of Cartago's hot springs were first discovered
by Spanish colonizers in the 1600s, who stumbled across a
beautiful mountain spring that produced clean, flowing hot
water. Reportedly, those who bathed in the spring's waters
noticed that they felt completely rejuvenated, with injuries
healed, and the signs of aging reversed. It was rumored that the
indigenous people who lived nearby had long been aware of

the hot spring's healing properties, and would carry water from the spring on long forest treks so that they could cure themselves of injuries or ailments. Some even believed that, if one drank from the springs every day, they would never age, and would be able to live forever. This led to the hot springs receiving the nickname – "The Fountain of Youth."

Between 1820 and 1910, the hot springs were a popular destination for those looking to improve their health, cure diseases, and heal injuries by bathing in or drinking the spring water. As word of the powers of the "Fountain of Youth" continued to spread, more and more visitors traveled to the area to see for themselves if the folklore had any truth to it. The Bella Vista resort, where tourists could bathe in the healing hot springs, became famous across Costa Rica as a popular destination for rest and relaxation. There were reports that the water in the springs had healed ailments including chronic skin conditions, arthritis, and autoimmune disease.

After an earthquake in 1910 caused severe damage to the surrounding area and its buildings, the Bella Vista resort was forced to close down. Over time, Cartago's hot springs were forgotten, fading into the background of history. They were recently rediscovered by a visiting restaurateur. After digging through rubble and waste to reach the long-buried springs,

Avraham Kolitzy sampled the water. He believed that the powers of the spring's water had not been exaggerated by history, and he personally attested to the healing powers and rejuvenating qualities of the water. Following the rediscovery of the hot springs, a resort and hotel were built on the surrounding land so that visitors to the area can experience the "Fountain of Youth" for themselves.

While there is currently no scientific evidence for why the waters of the hot spring seem to have such intense healing properties, the "Fountain of Youth" is certainly a worthwhile destination because of nothing more than the history of the springs. Whether you believe that the waters will heal you or not, the comfortable temperature of the thermal springs makes them a perfect place to bathe, relax, and rest.

ABOUT THE AUTHOR

Prateek Agrawal found a love for books at a young age. Growing up in a northern state of India, Prateek was most at home in a local library. Mystery and adventure books captivated him the most.

In middle school, he started writing short poems, only to keep them mostly to himself.

Now, he writes from his home in Costa Rica, where he lives with his wife.

Made in the USA
Coppell, TX
11 January 2024